D0599320

It's Check-up Time, Elmo!

Original story by Sarah Albee
Illustrated by Tom Brannon
Contributing writers: Elizabeth Clasing and P.J. Shaw

Dalmatian Press, LLC, 2005. All rights reserved.
Published by Dalmatian Press, LLC, 2005. The DALMATIAN PRESS name and logo are trademarks of Dalmatian Press, LLC, Franklin, Tennessee 37067. No part of this book may be reproduced or copied in any form without written permission from the copyright owner.

Printed in the U.S.A.
ISBN: 1-40371-608-0 (X) 1-40371-882-2 (M)

06 07 08 LBM 10 9 8 7 6 5 4 3 2
14266 Sesame Street 8x8 Storybook: It's Check-up Time, Elmo!

"Why is Elmo going to visit the doctor today?" Elmo asked one morning, as his mommy buckled the little monster into his car seat. "Elmo doesn't feel sick!"

"It's check-up time," Elmo's mommy reminded him. "You need a check-up even when you feel well. The doctor makes sure you're growing and staying healthy. She'll check your ears and eyes, and listen to your heart, too."

Elmo touched the fuzzy red fur over his heart. "Oooh! Elmo wonders what *that* sounds like."

"Today you'll find out," Mommy promised.

In the waiting room, Elmo saw a little green monster he knew.

"Lily! Are you here for a check-up, too?"

"No, I have a tummy ache," she said in a small voice, watching him play with some paper and crayons.

Elmo drew Lily a silly picture to make her smile.

"Will the doctor help Lily feel better?" Elmo asked his mommy.

"I'm sure she will," Mommy answered.

Just then, nurse Rhonda came in. Elmo liked her braided hair. Rhonda smiled a great big smile when she saw Elmo.

"Your turn next, Elmo!" she said.

Later, Elmo followed Rhonda into the examining room.

Rhonda smiled. "Hop up onto the scales, Elmo," she told him. "Let's see how much you've grown."

Rhonda was surprised at how much taller Elmo was since last time. "Elmo is a big monster now," he said happily.

Rhonda checked Elmo's eyes next.

Then she wrapped a cushion around Elmo's arm to test his blood pressure. He watched it puff up and down.

"Just like a balloon!" Elmo giggled.

After that, Dr. Diane came in. She asked Elmo about his pet fish, Dorothy, while she washed her hands.

"Maybe Dorothy needs a check-up, too," Elmo said. "Is there a doctor for fish?"

"Animal doctors are called veterinarians," said Dr. Diane. "But fish don't need check-ups like we do."

Elmo thought about that. "It would be hard to test Dorothy's ears and eyes. They're so tiny!"

"And I would need a scuba suit to give her a check-up," Dr. Diane said with a grin.

That made Elmo laugh!

Dr. Diane had a few more tests to give Elmo. She checked his reflexes first. The doctor tap-tap-tapped softly under Elmo's knee until his furry red leg suddenly jumped!

"Ha-ha! That feels so funny," Elmo giggled.

Then she took his temperature with a thermometer.

"Not too hot and not too cold," the doctor said with a smile. "Elmo is just right!"

The doctor checked Elmo's ears with a little light, then his throat. "Open wide, Elmo," she said. Elmo went "*aaah*."

Next, Dr. Diane asked him to lie down so she could feel his tummy for any aches.

It tickled a little! Elmo tried hard not to giggle until Dr. Diane was through.

Dr. Diane checked Elmo's back, and then said, "Time to listen to your breathing and your heart, Elmo."

"Yay! Elmo was wondering what a heart sounds like," Elmo exclaimed.

Dr. Diane listened with her stethoscope as Elmo took deep breaths. Then she moved it around to hear Elmo's heart. "This is what I hear," she said. "Thump-*thump*. Thump-*thump*. Thump-*thump*."

"Elmo's heart sounds like a drum!" said Elmo.

"That's right. Your heart sounds very strong," said Dr. Diane. "Run and play every day and it will get even stronger."

Elmo nodded happily. He could do that!

Finally, Dr. Diane asked Elmo some questions:
"Do you wear a bike helmet to stay healthy and safe? Do you ride in a car seat? Do you make sure a grown-up is watching when you go swimming or cross the street?"
Elmo answered yes to every one.

"And do you get plenty of rest?" the doctor asked Elmo.
He nodded. "Elmo does! And Elmo will make sure Mommy does, too."
Elmo's mommy laughed at that. "Thank you, Elmo," she said.

"Sometimes we need a shot during a check-up. The medicine keeps us safe from things that make us sick," Dr. Diane said. She looked into a folder with Elmo's name on it. "I see that you need one of those today, Elmo."

Elmo remembered getting a shot one time. He pointed to his arm. "It went right here," Elmo told nurse Rhonda. "It felt like a little pinch, that's all."

Elmo's mommy smiled proudly at Elmo while he got his shot.

"Dr. Diane is good at giving shots," she said, "but you were a very brave monster anyway, Elmo."

That made Elmo feel good. Then Elmo remembered something else. "Hey, Elmo got a sticker last time!"

Dr. Diane laughed. "You may have a special one today, too."

"Well, Elmo, that's it," said Dr. Diane. "We're done with your check-up."
Elmo waved good-bye happily. He liked knowing he was strong and healthy.
"Thanks, Dr. Diane," he said. "Elmo was feeling okay before his check-up, but
now Elmo feels even better!"

The End

Nurse Rhonda's Check-up Tips

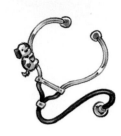

POSITIVE THOUGHTS Let your child know that doctors and nurses are there to help us feel better and to keep us healthy and strong!

INFORMATION Explain to your child that sometimes she will go to the doctor even when she feels okay, because regular check-ups help her stay healthy. You might say, "The nurse will call you from the waiting room and check your height, weight, blood pressure, and temperature. Later, the doctor will listen to your heart and lungs with a long, funny-looking instrument called a stethoscope, and examine your ears, nose, throat, and eyes with a light. The doctor might also check the reflexes in your knees with a little rubber hammer."

HONESTY It's important to be honest with your child about what he should expect during a doctor visit, even if it means talking about a shot. Say, "It may sting, but just for a little bit."

COMFORT Comforting words and actions are important, particularly if your child is injured or ill. Talk in a soothing voice and ask what would "make it better." Suggest that your child bring a doll or stuffed animal along on a visit to the doctor or hospital to make her feel more comfortable.

MAKE BELIEVE Pretending to be a doctor or nurse can help prepare a child for doctor visits. "Examine" the eyes, ears, and mouth of a favorite stuffed animal or doll, like Elmo. Encourage your child to take care of the toy by giving it lots of comfort and attention. Help tuck the doll into bed, for instance, and tell it to get lots of rest. Show your child how to blow the doll's nose, rub its tummy, and share a book. And ask some caring questions: "Did you eat a good breakfast today and drink lots of water? Did you take a nap? Will you come back for a check-up real soon?"

PRACTICE Help your child listen to your heart by hugging her close and placing her ear against your chest. Explain that a doctor or nurse will probably listen to her heart during a visit, but with a stethoscope.

"Elmo loves getting a check-up, and Elmo loves YOU!"